ANIMAL JAM

CALL

OF THE

ALPHAS

BY ELLIS BYRD

Penguin Young Readers Licenses
An Imprint of Penguin Random House

PENGUIN YOUNG READERS LICENSES
An Imprint of Penguin Random House LLC

Cover illustrated by Jemma Kemker

ISBN 9780451534477   10 9 8 7 6 5 4 3 2 1

PROLOGUE

A LONG tiME aGO . . .

All across the land, the animals of Jamaa were celebrating.

In Appondale, the hot sun beat down on several elephants rolling around happily in the mud pool. Around them, giraffes stretched their necks to reach the leaves at the top of the highest acacia trees. Cheetahs raced across the grass, chasing the elephants in game after game of tag.

Shimmering snow fell gently on Mt. Shiveer, covering the ski tracks the penguins and pandas left on the slopes. In a cozy hut near the top of the mountain, snow leopards and arctic wolves toasted their friendship with steaming mugs of hot cocoa.

The normally quiet Sarepia Forest was alive with music as bunnies thumped their feet in rhythm while lions provided a bass line. Raccoons danced and twirled in the clearing, and soon even the wolves gave in and joined the frolicking.

In Kimbara Outback, kangaroos cooled off in the clear streams running out from the great reservoir, laughing and splashing one another. Nearby, some koalas napped while others leisurely munched away at an all-you-can-eat eucalyptus-leaf buffet.

Horses galloped up the rocky trails of

Coral Canyons to join the foxes and lions around a crackling campfire. The sun began to set, causing the mesa surrounding them to glow red and orange. A few eagles soaring overhead dipped lower to listen as the foxes told tale after tale.

Although they celebrated in different ways, the animals were all rejoicing for the same reason. They enjoyed a deep connection to their land and strong friendships with one another. And to strengthen this, each species had just received an incredible gift from the guardian spirits of Jamaa: a Heartstone.

"Your Heartstone contains the essence of your species," Mira had told them, spreading her great heron wings and ruffling her blue-gray feathers. Her eyes shone with pride, and her long beak curved in a gentle smile. "It contains what makes you special . . . the secret of what makes you who you are."

"They're beautiful," said a panda, his eyes wide with awe.

A raccoon nodded in agreement. "But what if we lose them?" she fretted. "How can we keep them safe?"

Zios answered, his expression radiating warmth. "Mira and I have a place in mind to store all the Heartstones together." The guardian spirit looked down at the animals through his golden mask.

"All together?" asked a wolf, arching his brow.

Mira nodded. "They'll be safe there. We promise."

The animals agreed, and so the two guardian spirits of Jamaa hid the

Heartstones beneath the Lost Temple of Zios, an ancient temple that had stood in the jungle for as long as anyone could remember. And for many years afterward, animals across the land continued to live in peace and harmony.

But as time went on, seeds of suspicion began to bloom in their hearts. The cheetahs became convinced the tigers envied their speed. The nervous raccoons told themselves the wolves looked rather shifty. The foxes' tall tales began to irritate the lions, who were starting to think foxes lied a little too naturally. Soon, not a single species trusted another.

The wolves were the first to remove their Heartstone from beneath the Lost Temple of Zios. The others soon followed their example, bringing their Heartstones to their individual villages, and the camaraderie between the animals of Jamaa was lost.

It was during this time of division that a new threat began to creep its slimy tentacles into Jamaa: a horde of evil Phantoms. They were led by the cruel Phantom Queen, and no one in Jamaa had ever seen such vile creatures. The Phantoms spread filth and pollution all over the land, and as they did, rumors about their intentions began to spread as well.

"They're poisoning the water," one monkey informed another over a murky watering hole. "To make us sick."

"They're polluting the air," a kangaroo croaked after a long coughing fit. "To make us leave."

"They're not just ruining our environment," a tiger realized somberly. "They're making it hospitable for *themselves*. They want to take over Jamaa."

Before long, the Phantoms set their sights on the Heartstones. Not only did they take over the animals' villages and steal the precious jewels, the Phantoms turned their power to a darker purpose: using each Heartstone to trap its entire species.

One by one, the animals vanished: the kangaroos, the lions, the raccoons, the elephants, the cheetahs. And with every disappearance, all the other species withdrew even more, trusting no one but themselves.

Although Mira and Zios were powerful guardians, even they could not stop the

Phantoms' progress. And before they knew it, there were only six Heartstones—and six species—left in Jamaa.

CHAPTER ONE

Mira soared through the sky, surveying the land she loved in dismay. Most of Jamaa was polluted almost beyond recognition. The crisp, fresh air of Sarepia Forest was now heavy with gray smog that caused the giant green trees to shrivel and turn brown. The clear waters of Crystal Reef were murky and muddy, and the majestic glaciers of Mt. Shiveer had begun to melt.

Worst of all, the sounds of life that

once filled every corner of the land were all but gone. Mira's heart ached as she remembered the splashing dolphins in Kani Cove, the galloping horses of Coral Canyons, and the peaceful sloths that used to inhabit the lush jungle surrounding the Lost Temple of Zios. There had been so many wonderfully different species, all sharing Jamaa and living in harmony.

"It's hard to believe this is the same land," Mira said when Zios appeared at her side. "How can we possibly reverse all the destruction the Phantoms have caused?"

"I don't think we can," Zios replied, his voice deep with sadness. "At least, not while the Phantoms continue spreading their pollution . . . and stealing Heartstones. I fear they will soon be the only creatures left."

Mira sighed, contemplating the barren

land below them. "We can't allow that to happen," she said determinedly. "There are still animals in Jamaa. This is their rightful land."

"It is," Zios agreed. "But you know they're in hiding. Their only concern is protecting the Heartstones."

Mira arched her slender neck, the sunlight making her feathers sparkle. "I know the Phantoms are powerful. But, Zios, we accomplished so many incredible things when the species all lived and worked together, remember?" She sighed wistfully. "There was no challenge that couldn't be met. If the remaining animals could unite once more, the way they used to . . ."

Zios knew what Mira was thinking. "They just might be able to take Jamaa back from the Phantoms," he finished. He closed his eyes and concentrated, then turned to his companion. "I think you're right, Mira. It's our best chance—and theirs. We must try."

And so the two guardian spirits of Jamaa called the remaining six species of animals together: pandas, monkeys, koalas, bunnies, tigers, and wolves. Volunteers from each species gathered at the Lost Temple of Zios, pawing the ground, peering out from the bushes, hanging from branches, eyes darting around suspiciously. The animals were eager to reclaim their land, but their mistrust of one another was obvious. Especially when it came to their Heartstones.

Zios solemnly moved from one group to the next, collecting the Heartstones. Although the species were reluctant to part with the precious stones, one by one they handed them over to the guardian spirit Zios. Only once he had stored them in a safe place did the animals turn their attention to Mira.

"Animals of Jamaa," the heron called, her voice ringing around the clearing. "We know you have your differences. But it is time to set those aside, for you have a common foe."

A few of the animals murmured in agreement. Others looked more doubtful, but listened intently.

"The Phantoms have poisoned our land," Zios rumbled. "But it's not too late. It *is* possible for us to defeat this enemy . . . by working *together*."

A high-pitched, hissing laugh caused all the animals to startle and look around.

A Phantom appeared from behind a wilting silk-cotton tree and glided through the clearing. He had four spindly tentacles on each side like a spider, and the pupil of his eye was extra tiny and beady. Several of the animals growled and glared, but the Phantom responded with an evil sneer that caused even the wolves to fall silent.

"My name is Leach," he said, his voice slithering in and out of their ears like a snake. "And this is Stench." A second Phantom appeared behind the bunnies, sniggering when they jumped in fright. Stench had two large, lumbering tentacles that seemed too big for his body, and several smaller tentacles that waved uselessly on top of his head. He tried to glare at the animals as menacingly as Leach, but one tiny tentacle fell limp in front of his eye. Stench batted it away with a bigger tentacle and accidentally poked himself in the pupil.

"Ow," he mumbled. A few bunnies tittered, and Leach's eye narrowed.

"We have a message from the Phantom Queen," Leach announced, his voice soft but menacing. The giggling stopped abruptly. "She knows what you are planning, and she knows you will not succeed."

Stench continued, "You believe we Phantoms are the problem. But the truth is, Jamaa's problems began before our arrival. They began . . . with you."

Mira and Zios exchanged a worried look. But before they could respond, a koala piped up.

"He's talking about the wolves!" he cried accusingly. "We all know the wolves are responsible for letting the Phantoms into this land to begin with."

A tiger tossed his head. "That may be so, but you koalas and your laziness helped the Phantoms take over, despite the valiant effort of *my* species to defend our land."

"You tigers are so arrogant. You don't know what the rest of us have done to try to protect Jamaa," a monkey called out from where she dangled from a particularly high branch. "Although at least you're willing to fight. Unlike the bunnies, who just turn their fuzzy little tails and run."

The bunnies hopped up and down and shook their fists angrily. The tigers pawed the ground. The wolves huddled closer together, hackles raised and teeth bared. Mira and Zios looked on helplessly.

Leach cackled and hissed. "Quite an army you've put together, oh great guardian spirits of Jamaa," he told them, his eye flashing darkly. "Now, let's see how they fight."

Suddenly, the leaves rustled and the bushes shook. The bickering animals fell silent as a blue-white electric glow began to grow all around them.

"Attack!" Stench bellowed, flapping his lumbering tentacles and nearly knocking Leach over. Dozens of Phantoms emerged from the shadows and swarmed into the clearing. Chaos erupted.

Overhead, the monkeys frantically began to build a net from leaves and vines. "Hey!" one yelped as a koala snatched the vine from his hands.

"We should use these as lassos!" the

koala cried. "That would be much more useful than a net!"

Their argument was drowned out by the mighty roars of the tigers, who charged headfirst into battle without looking to see what the other species were doing. The wolves prowled around on the outskirts, watching and waiting.

"Join us, you cowards!" one tiger called. "Or do you not know which side you're fighting for?"

"It's foolish to engage with an enemy you know little about," a wolf replied with a sneer. "But go ahead with your blind attack so we can learn what *doesn't* work."

A few pandas surrounded one of the Phantoms. "Maybe we can talk about this," one began, paws raised in a peaceful gesture. But with lightning-fast speed, several bunnies hopped into attack mode, waving sticks and leaping between the pandas and the Phantom.

The Phantoms saw the divisiveness between all the species and used it to their advantage. Their tentacles twirled rapidly, and they hacked at the vines until they fell, tangling the koalas and monkeys in their own lassos and nets. They allowed the tigers to chase them over to the wolves, and then levitated into the air, watching as the two species clashed with each other. They burned the leaves of the silk-cotton tree until the bunnies couldn't see through the smoke, causing them to surround the pandas instead.

In all the confusion, no one noticed Leach slipping into the entrance of one of the stone buildings. He soon emerged carrying a gleaming jewel. The sparkle caught Mira's eye, and she gasped.

"He has a Heartstone!"

Her otherworldly cry seemed to almost shimmer in the air, rising like a song above the sounds of battle. Snarling, a wolf leaped toward Leach just as a monkey swung down and snatched the Heartstone. Leach shifted nimbly out of the way, and the wolf tumbled to the ground with the monkey in his paws.

"Get off, wolf!" the monkey cried, dropping the Heartstone and leaping back up into the trees. Suddenly, a blinding light emanated from the center of the turmoil. Shielding his eye, Leach slipped back into the jungle, followed by Stench and the rest of the Phantoms. Confused and frightened, the other animals fled in different directions.

When the sounds of the stampede had faded, the bright light dimmed and disappeared to reveal Zios standing guard over the Heartstone lying in the grass. He examined it as Mira joined him.

"The tigers," he said gravely. "This is their Heartstone. The battle was just a distraction. Leach must have intended on stealing it while the others were fighting."

Mira's feathers rustled in the breeze. "Fighting against one another instead of against the Phantoms," she replied. "Leach was right. The problems in Jamaa began before the Phantoms arrived, when the species stopped trusting one another. And they *still* don't trust each other. If we're ever going to restore this land, they must regain that trust. But how will we ever do that?"

"They need to see proof," Zios replied thoughtfully. "Proof that they can put their faith in each other. Proof that they're stronger when they're united. They need leaders."

Mira continued Zios's train of thought. "Six leaders, one representing each species, all working together and combining their powers. And then, if they can convince the other animals to join them . . . ," she said, a smile forming.

Zios's eyes glimmered. "Then surely they can drive the Phantoms out once and for all!"

Mira stretched her wings gracefully. "What are we waiting for? Let's find the leaders who will save Jamaa!"

CHAPTER TWO

The guardian spirits of Jamaa had just reached the outskirts of the jungle when they heard a rumbling noise. Up ahead, Mira spotted a few sparks shooting out from a particularly large patch of smog.

"More Phantoms?" she asked warily.

Zios was silent for a moment. "I don't think so," he replied at last. "It looks as if the smog is . . . disappearing? Do you see that?"

"I do!"

The thick gray clouds swirled down from the tops of the trees, winding around the branches like liquid through a curly straw. Mira and Zios hurried forward, and as they drew nearer to the source of the sparks, the rumbling noise grew louder and louder.

"My goodness!" Mira cried, coming to a halt at the edge of a small clearing. "Look at that!"

At the center of the clearing sat a bizarre-looking contraption. The engine was covered in copper coils and bamboo tubes. As Mira and Zios watched in astonishment, the tubes sucked the smog right out of the air.

A monkey with a shock of white hair and a beard to match darted out from behind the machine, prodding the tubes and wiggling the coils. When the last of the smog was gone, the monkey grabbed hold of a large lever and pulled it down. The contraption sputtered and sparked for a few more seconds, then fell still.

"Marvelous!" Mira exclaimed, and the monkey jumped, clearly startled. "Did you build this machine yourself?"

"Yes, yes indeed," the monkey replied, adjusting his goggles. "It's a smog vacuum! Only instead of containing the smog in a bag like a regular vacuum, it filters the smog into clean air, expelled here." He pointed at a single long bamboo tube jutting out below the lever, then frowned thoughtfully. "Hmm. Perhaps I should give it a different name. Smog cleaner? Smog purifier? Smog . . . spick-and-spanner?"

"Whatever you choose to call it, it's a

brilliant invention," Zios said. "What's your name, my friend?"

"Thank you, thank you! I'm Graham. And you're . . ." The monkey squinted. "Why, you're the guardian spirits of Jamaa!"

Mira smiled. "Indeed. And it's a pleasure to meet you, Graham."

"The pleasure is all mine. Oh dear, looks like that bolt's come loose . . ." Picking up a small wrench that had been lying in the grass, Graham began tightening the bolt. "I based the design on a snowblower I built ages ago to clear trails around Mt. Shiveer. See?" He pulled a photo from his belt and waved it at them. "The wolves had been digging paths, always digging, digging, digging. Rather the hard way to do it, don't you think? So much work! By the time they'd reach the end of the path, snow was already piling up again at the beginning. They just went round and round. Might as well be chasing their tails!"

"The work you put into keeping Jamaa clean and safe is admirable," Mira said, examining the gadget in the photo. "Many animals have given up, thanks to the Phantoms."

Graham was still inspecting his smog vacuum. "No sense in giving up, none at all," he said distractedly. "There are still some natural resources at hand, aren't there? Whatever's available is all I need, that's what I always say."

Mira and Zios exchanged a smile.

"Graham," Mira said. "We have a proposition for you."

The guardian spirits explained their

plan to Graham, who listened curiously. Once they finished, he clapped his hands in delight.

"Just tell me where and when the meeting is, and I'll be there!" Graham said, snapping his goggles back into place. "Glad that panda gave me this photo. Reminded me of my own invention!"

"Who is this panda?" Zios asked.

Graham scratched his head. "Lily? Leela? Loo-Loo? Can't remember. An explorer, though, that I do recall. She's been trekking all over Jamaa, documenting with her camera the destruction the Phantoms have caused. Still at Mt. Shiveer, I believe."

Mira and Zios left Graham tinkering with his smog vacuum and continued their search for leaders. "Let's find this panda," Mira said. "If she really is that knowledgeable about the Phantoms' destruction, she could be a great asset to our team."

When they arrived at the base of Mt. Shiveer, they found two wolves arguing with a bunny near a fork in the path.

"The hot springs are next to our village," one of the wolves snapped. "That makes them our territory."

"I've got no interest in your territory," the bunny sniffed. "I just . . . ah . . . ahhh*CHOO*!"

The other wolf stepped to the side, blocking the path uphill. "Well, that's it. You're not getting anywhere near our village now, not if you're sick."

As the three continued to bicker, a panda with bright purple eyes strolled down the path from the hot springs. She stopped when she reached the wolves, leaning on her long wooden staff and smiling.

"Excuse me," she said cheerfully. "I'd like to pass, please."

The wolves glanced at each other, then grudgingly stepped aside. "Sorry, Liza," one mumbled.

"Ahhh*CHOO*!"

Liza turned to the bunny. "Goodness! That's quite a cold you have. Are you on your way to the hot springs?"

"I was," the bunny grumbled, shivering. "But these two claim it's their territory."

"He's contagious!" one of the wolves told Liza defensively. "We just don't want his germs near our village."

"But surely you realize he has every right to visit the springs," Liza said, pulling a small bottle from the pocket of her belt. "And as for that cold, I think this just might do the trick!"

She handed the bottle to the bunny, who sipped the contents tentatively. He blinked, a smile spreading across his face. "Wow, I feel better already! What is this stuff?"

"A special potion made with eucalyptus oil," Liza replied. "Enjoy the hot springs!"

The wolves stood reluctantly aside, allowing the bunny to hop up the path. Mira and Zios waited near a grayish melting snowbank as Liza drew nearer. The panda paused when she spotted them, her mouth forming a round O of surprise.

"Oh my goodness!" she exclaimed. "You're . . . you're Mira and Zios! The guardian spirits!"

"Hello, Liza," said Mira warmly. "It's

a pleasure to meet you. We couldn't help overhearing what just happened."

"You did a remarkable job handling that disagreement," Zios continued. "Would you be interested in taking on a greater role to unite the animals of Jamaa?"

Liza's purple eyes widened. "Unite the animals of Jamaa? Of course, but . . . but how? What role could I possibly play?"

"The role of a leader," Zios replied, and Liza gripped her wooden staff even tighter.

"A leader? Oh my . . ." Liza took a deep breath. "I'm honored. May I have some time to consider it?"

"Of course," Mira replied. "We'll send word soon with a time and location for a meeting. Also, may I ask where you acquired that eucalyptus potion?"

"I got it in Kimbara Outback," Liza told

her. "The pollution in that area has caused all sorts of strange sicknesses among the poor koalas. Luckily, a brilliant young healer recently arrived to help them. He's got a special gift for working with plants."

Mira ruffled her wings and turned to Zios. "Perhaps we should meet this healer."

After bidding Liza goodbye, the guardian spirits of Jamaa set off for Kimbara Outback. The air grew warmer during their journey, but the sun remained hidden behind a dense haze.

Mira coughed. "The smog," she told Zios morosely. "It's getting thicker."

They arrived at Kimbara Outback to find dozens of koalas lined up outside a makeshift tent, some hopping and twitching in agitation. Behind them, the dry grass stretched out as far as the eye could see and was covered in oily streaks of brownish black that zigzagged the horizon.

"This itch is unbearable," one koala moaned, hopping from one swollen foot to the other. Another nodded, scratching her red ears compulsively.

"The Phantoms," Mira sighed. "Their effect here is even worse than I feared."

Before Zios could respond, a high-pitched cackle of delight came from the tent.

"I've got it! I've done it!" A koala in a moss skirt bounded outside, gleefully waving two large bottles over his head. "The cinchona trees, of course! I collected the leaves ages ago, and this lotion will do the trick! On your *feet*! On your *ears*! On your *nose*! On your *elbow*! Even in between your *toes*!"

As he spoke, he danced down the line of koalas, slathering lotion onto their rashes. Each koala wore a momentary look of surprise before laughing in relief.

"Thanks, Cosmo!" the last koala called, wiggling her ears. Cosmo waved goodbye with his empty bottles, then headed back into the tent, where Mira and Zios were waiting.

"Oh!" Cosmo cried, nearly dropping his bottles. "Aren't you . . ."

"The guardian spirits of Jamaa, yes," Mira replied kindly, and she explained their plan for the third time.

"I'd be *thrilled* to help!" Cosmo exclaimed. "The plants are on our side, you know. I've heard them whispering to each other about the Phantoms, about Jamaa. If the animals work with one

another—and with the plants, of course—
we can restore this land to what it was . . .
just like it used to be!"

He pointed to a painting near the back
of the tent. Red-orange land dotted with
colorful shrubs sparkled under a clear,
deep blue sky. Tears welled up in Mira's
eyes as she stepped closer.

"This is what Kimbara Outback looked
like before the Phantoms," she said softly.
"It's beautiful. And look, here's the artist's
signature: Peck."

"A bunny, I believe," Cosmo said,
grabbing a handful of leaves from a nearby
tree. "One of the other healers got it from
the Art Studio in Coral Canyons."

The guardian spirits wasted no time.
After promising to contact Cosmo soon,
they hurried to Coral Canyons. Mira

was dismayed to see the oily streaks covered many of the once beautiful red rocks as well.

"Is there no place in Jamaa the Phantoms haven't touched?" she wondered. "This is . . . Oh! Zios, look at that!"

Below, a group of bunnies were gathered in front of an enormous flat-faced rock that had been scrubbed clean of oil. Each bunny held a chunk of something grayish black, which they were using to sketch and scribble on the pale sandstone.

"Are they drawing?" Mira asked, edging closer quietly so as not to disturb their work.

"Indeed," Zios murmured. "It's a mural . . . of the Lost Temple of Zios."

As they watched, a bunny with light pink and purple fur bounced around the group, calling instructions.

"Beautiful, beautiful!" she cried. "Now let's add the tree along the east side. Giant, huge! With thick vines! And there's the river, too, can't forget the river . . ."

Mira smiled. "I believe we've found Peck."

Peck's right ear twitched, causing her yellow bell earring to jingle. "Did I hear my name?" she asked, turning around. Her violet eyes widened in surprise. "M-Mira! And Zios! Oh my!"

"We're admirers of your work, Peck," Mira told her. "Your painting of Kimbara Outback is stunning. And this mural is incredible."

"Thank you!" Peck replied, blushing. "There was a fire recently in Sarepia Forest, and I thought I might as well put the charcoal to good use. The destruction of so many trees had everyone really down, and I wanted to show them that you can find beauty in anything."

"So you're creating a mural of Jamaa," Mira said. "The old Jamaa, before the Phantoms."

"Oh no." Peck's eyes flashed. "This is the *future* Jamaa. It will look like this again one day. I have to believe that."

"As do we," Zios said, pleased. "And you can help us ensure that it happens."

"I can?"

Mira nodded. "We're looking for six leaders, one to represent each of Jamaa's remaining species, to help unite all the animals in the fight against the Phantoms."

Peck's ears flattened against her head. "And you think I can be a—a leader?"

"Of course!" Zios said, a laugh in his voice. "Just look at what you've accomplished already!"

The three turned to look at the mural. Two bunnies were busily sketching differently shaped jewels, all clustered together near the bottom of the drawing.

"The Heartstones!" Mira said in wonder. "All together and safe, the way they once were."

Peck nodded, her bell jangling again. "When we were gathering the charcoal, we met a tiger whose den is just on the outskirts of the fire. He was very curious about what we were doing, and he ended up telling us the story of the Heartstones while we worked."

Zios glanced at Mira, a question in his eyes, and Mira nodded in silent agreement. After thanking Peck and promising to be in touch soon, they hastened to Sarepia Forest. The fire-damaged area was easy to find. Any trees left standing were charred and leafless, and smoke still lingered in the air. The guardian spirits of Jamaa soon found the den that Peck had mentioned.

Inside, they found fire flickering in a cozy stone hearth, a kettle hanging just above the flames. A large tiger with a braided beard was curled up nearby, studying a map intently. He looked up when Mira stepped forward, and quickly stood.

"Good heavens!"

"We're sorry to disturb you," Mira began. "I am Mira, and this is Zios."

"The guardian spirits of Jamaa, of course," the tiger replied with a regal bow.

"I am Sir Gilbert. It's an honor to meet you both."

They gathered around the hearth, and once Sir Gilbert had poured them all a cup of tea, Mira explained their plan yet again.

Sir Gilbert regarded her thoughtfully when she'd finished. "So you've found leaders for the monkeys, pandas, koalas, and bunnies?"

"We have," Zios confirmed. "And we were hoping you might lead your species in this endeavor."

"I'm humbled by your request," Sir Gilbert replied, lifting his head. "Of course, I am willing to do whatever is necessary to defeat the Phantoms. And I do think this plan has merit. However . . ."

"Yes?" Mira prompted.

Sir Gilbert sighed. "These other four

leaders you've recruited sound worthy of the task ahead. But if you truly mean to have a leader for each species involved in this endeavor, I must say I have a few reservations about letting a wolf into the fold."

"But we must," Mira said firmly. "The only way the animals of Jamaa will succeed in reclaiming their land is if they work together—*all* of them. Just as it was before."

Several seconds of silence passed as Sir Gilbert considered this. "All right," he said at last, nodding. "I see your point, and I agree. But I implore you," he added, his expression grave. "Please take great care in choosing the leader of the wolves. They can be quite crafty."

"Indeed they can," Mira agreed,

smiling. "And that is exactly the quality we're looking for."

"We'll contact you soon," Zios told Sir Gilbert. The guardian spirits nodded at the tiger and departed.

Neither spoke until they had retreated deep into the dark, quiet forest. Then Mira stopped and sighed.

"I meant what I said," she told Zios solemnly. "We absolutely must have a leader for the wolves. But I know the other leaders will share Sir Gilbert's reservations. How will we find the *right* wolf for the job?"

Zios had closed his eyes as Mira spoke. "Perhaps," he said in a low voice, "the right wolf has already found *us*."

Mira tilted her head, confused. Then the feathers along her back prickled and fluttered, and she turned to see a pair of yellow eyes peering at them from the shadows between the trees.

The guardian spirits watched and waited in silence. A moment later, a blue-gray wolf stepped out from the dark. Mira studied him appraisingly.

"Have you been following us since we left Sir Gilbert's?" she asked.

"Longer." The wolf's gruff voice was so low, it was barely audible over the wind through the leaves. "I've been tracking Leach and Stench since the battle, and I crossed your path a few times on your quest."

"What is your name?"

The wolf eyed her, his reluctance to answer evident. "Greely," he said at last.

Mira nodded. "So, Greely, may I assume

you know about our plan already?"

Greely gave a short nod. "I do, but Sir Gilbert speaks the truth. This isn't something anyone would want the wolves involved in—and that includes the wolves." He paused, sniffing. "We work better on our own. Myself especially."

"I don't doubt you are a skilled tracker," Mira said. "But how do you know you wouldn't be even better as part of a team if you've never tried it?"

Zios chimed in. "We believe that working together will give the animals of Jamaa their best chance at defeating the Phantoms. But of course, each animal has to make that choice."

"We'll send word about the meeting soon." Mira paused, holding Greely's gaze. "Will you at least consider it until then?"

Greely sat silently, the wind ruffling his fur. At last, he nodded. "I'll consider it."

He slipped back into the darkness of the forest, leaving the guardian spirits of Jamaa staring after him uncertainly.

CHAPTER THREE

In a remote part of Jamaa, hidden from
nearby villages in a tightly packed thicket,
was a small clearing with a magnificent
tree in its center. The tree didn't so much
have a trunk as it did dozens of thick
roots twisting up out of the ground and
wrapping closely around one another.
Together, they stretched up into the
sky before splitting into hundreds of
branches that hung high overhead, heavy

with enormous green leaves.

Mira and Zios waited beneath its canopy. Liza was the first to arrive, immediately pulling out her camera and snapping photo after photo of the tree. Cosmo and Peck showed up at the same time, both bouncing with excitement. While Peck marveled at the size of each leaf—sturdy enough for a canvas, she exclaimed ecstatically—Cosmo pressed his ear to the knotted trunk and laughed with delight, almost as if the tree had told him a joke.

Sir Gilbert appeared next, and he watched the others' antics with obvious amusement. A loud rumbling, rattling sound announced Graham's arrival, and the sight of his smog vacuum bursting out of the bushes sent Peck scurrying behind the tree in fright. Liza marveled over the contraption, while Cosmo and Sir Gilbert looked on from a distance with mixed expressions of curiosity and suspicion.

Arching her neck, Mira peered through the surrounding trees. "How much longer should we give Greely?" she murmured to Zios. Before he could respond, Sir Gilbert lifted his head sharply, and his eyes narrowed at a cluster of brambly bushes near the tree.

"Show yourself, wolf!" he called out, his tone commanding. After a moment, Greely stepped out of the bushes. He eyed Sir Gilbert disdainfully, and the tiger regarded him with equal derision. A chilly hush fell over the animals as they watched Greely approach the tree.

"Welcome, Greely," Mira said warmly.

"I'm so glad you decided to join us." Greely bowed his head in acknowledgment, but didn't respond. When he passed the smog vacuum, Graham stepped in front of it protectively, mumbling something under his breath. Cosmo and Peck edged away nervously, whispering to each other when Greely reached the group. Liza attempted to smile at the wolf, but he ignored her.

"Thank you all for coming." Zios's deep rumbling voice, though kind, caused the animals to fall silent immediately. "As you know, we've called you here because the Phantoms' grip on Jamaa is only growing more suffocating."

"Since our last battle with the Phantoms, we have traveled all over this land to find the leaders necessary to defeat them," Mira continued. "And we've seen just how terrible the extent of the Phantoms' destruction has become. The jungles are filled with smog. The oily dirt in the plains is causing rashes and illness. The snow in the mountains is gray slush. The forests have suffered yet another fire. And it's only getting worse."

As she spoke, the animals listened intently. Greely and Liza looked unsurprised but disturbed, while Sir Gilbert's brow was furrowed in concentration. Cosmo tilted his head, and Graham glanced forlornly at his smog vacuum. Peck's eyes had filled with tears, but she kept her chin up determinedly.

"We need the six of you if we're going to defeat the Phantoms," Zios told them. "As leaders—as *Alphas*—you are the key to driving the Phantoms from this land

and healing our damaged world. To help with this endeavor, Mira and I have a gift for you."

Mira swept a wing across the grass, and six glittering jewels appeared, sparkling among the blades. Cosmo and Peck edged forward eagerly to take a better look.

"These are your Alpha Stones," Mira explained. "Six jewels with restorative properties that work with the natural world. They can also harness and amplify each of your unique powers. Like healing and creativity," she said with a smile, handing Cosmo and Peck their gems.

"Diplomacy and strategy," Zios continued, presenting Liza and Sir Gilbert with two more jewels.

"Ingenuity," Mira went on, handing a jewel to Graham. "And perception." She offered the final Alpha Stone to Greely, who hesitated for a moment before accepting it.

"Thank you," Peck said, her voice trembling a bit with excitement and nerves. "Do you really think the six of us can defeat all the Phantoms?"

"We believe you can do more than that," Zios replied. "We believe you can unify all your species in this fight. And . . ."

He glanced at Mira, who stood taller and surveyed the Alphas.

"And we believe you can find the Heartstones the Phantoms stole and bring back the lost species," she finished.

Even Greely had difficulty hiding his surprise. A smile spread slowly across Liza's face, and Peck's eyes shone with wonder. Sir Gilbert stepped forward, his head held high.

"I think we can all agree that would be marvelous," he said. "And I for one am willing to work together to accomplish this goal."

He smiled around at the other animals, though he didn't quite meet Greely's eyes.

"I'm glad to hear it," Mira said. "And now, we'd like to welcome you to Alphas Hollow."

She and Zios moved aside, and the animals stared curiously at the twisting trunk of the massive tree. As they watched, the roots shifted and writhed until an opening appeared. Sir Gilbert stepped inside first, closely followed by Liza and Cosmo. Peck waited for Graham to push his smog vacuum inside.

"Aren't you coming?" she asked Greely, who hadn't budged. The wolf didn't respond at first, but Peck continued to smile hopefully at him. Finally, he sighed.

"Yes. After you, of course."

Ears twitching, Peck hopped through the entrance, Greely right behind her. Mira and Zios entered last, and the roots drew together once more, closing behind them.

They watched, pleased, as the Alphas exclaimed over the interior. Enormous, intricate maps of the diverse lands and oceans of Jamaa covered any available wall space. Potted plants sat in the corners and hung from the ceiling, each containing various herbs and flowers that filled the Hollow with a sharp woodsy scent. A fire crackled merrily in a hearth on the right wall, along with a huge cabinet filled with every type of tool imaginable. On the opposite wall were shelves stocked with colorful paints, pencils, and brushes.

In the center of the Hollow sat a giant round table, six cushions evenly spaced around it. Greely watched the others marvel over the space from his spot near the entrance, his expression inscrutable.

"We hope this place will serve as a useful headquarters," Mira announced. "As you can see, there are plenty of resources here to help you formulate a plan to defeat the Phantoms."

"It's wonderful," Cosmo said, dried dandelions clutched in his paws. Nearby, Graham nearly dropped a monkey wrench as he nodded fervently in agreement.

Zios's eyes glowed. "Excellent. Now that

you are all together, Mira and I must be on our way."

"Already?" Peck cried.

Mira nodded gravely. "Until our search for the six of you, we hadn't realized just how dire Jamaa's environmental problems are. The melting snowbanks, the oily sand, the smog . . . We need to survey the land extensively to see just how far the damage has spread."

Cosmo opened his mouth to protest, but Sir Gilbert spoke first.

"Thank you both," he said, his voice deep yet soft. "We won't let you down."

Mira's wings fluttered. "We know," she replied. "That's why we chose you."

And with that, the guardian spirits of Jamaa departed, leaving the Alphas alone in the Hollow.

CHAPTER FOUR

Inside Alphas Hollow, the silence was long and uncomfortable. Finally, Sir Gilbert approached the giant round table, gesturing to the cushions with his paw.

"Shall we?"

The others obeyed immediately, scurrying to take a seat. Peck and Cosmo claimed the thickest, tallest cushions, which helped them see over the table. Liza sat cross-legged on a flat turquoise pillow, while Graham climbed onto a stiff straw cushion with squat wooden legs. Sir Gilbert claimed a velvet maroon-and-gold mat, then coughed expectantly, eyeing the entrance.

Greely had not budged from his spot. The other animals watched anxiously as he stood slowly, almost defiantly, and headed toward the table. He stopped next to a cushion woven from thin blades of grass, but did not sit.

Sir Gilbert placed his Alpha Stone on the table, where it glittered brightly. "Mira said these stones can harness our unique abilities and amplify them, making us more powerful," he began slowly. "I propose we start there. Our plan should play to each of our individual strengths."

"I agree," Liza said, placing her

own Alpha Stone on the table. "One of our biggest challenges is going to be convincing all the species to trust one another again. I can go to Jamaa Township and start talking to them. Maybe if they hear about the way we're working together, it will give them hope, and they can begin to build trust as well."

"Excellent idea," Sir Gilbert said approvingly. "Now, which areas of Jamaa are hurting most? The rest of us should probably begin our efforts there."

"Kimbara Outback," Cosmo piped up. "It's not just the oily dirt. What little water the area had is nearly gone."

Sir Gilbert sighed. "The Phantoms' work, I would venture to guess." He looked from Cosmo to Graham. "Why don't the two of you go there together? Cosmo, you know the area, and perhaps Graham can put his inventive skills to work helping the inhabitants of Kimbara Outback find water in the meantime."

Cosmo eyed Graham doubtfully, but nodded in agreement. "Okay!"

"Appondale is also suffering," Liza informed the others. She pulled out the photos she had taken for them to see. "The mud hole is nearly dried up, and the baobab trees are dying. One of the local tigers told me the trees aren't able to store water the way they used to."

"Hmm," Sir Gilbert said thoughtfully. "Perhaps I should visit my fellow tigers and learn more about these problems."

"Can I come with you?" Peck asked earnestly. "I studied the baobab trees for a woodworking craft project once. I might be able to help come up with a solution."

Sir Gilbert smiled and bowed his head. "I would be honored to have you as a traveling companion," he replied, and Peck giggled at his formality.

Liza cleared her throat. "And what about you, Greely?" she asked. "Would you like to accompany me to Jamaa Township? A panda and a wolf working side by side would be a real demonstration of cooperation the other animals might appreciate."

"Perhaps," Greely said, arching one white eyebrow. "But I prefer not to have a partner. Rest assured, I'll do my part."

Turning, he headed for the door. Peck's mouth fell open, and Sir Gilbert's eyes flashed dangerously.

"And what exactly *is* your part?" he called after Greely. The wolf paused and surveyed the rest of the Alphas, his expression unreadable.

"You heard Mira," he said. "My strongest asset to this group is my perception, an awareness of what is going on around me." He continued walking toward the door. "I can do the same for us . . . but only on my terms."

With that, Greely left Alphas Hollow. Several seconds passed in silence as the other Alphas looked at one another nervously.

"I suppose there's no sense in delaying," Sir Gilbert said at last, rising from his cushion. "Our mission awaits!"

Hours later, Sir Gilbert and Peck had just reached the outskirts of Appondale.

Peck was enjoying the journey; Sir Gilbert's formality had been a little intimidating at first, but he was actually quite warm and inquisitive. She told him tale after tale about her adventures, the Art Studio, and even the mural in progress back in Coral Canyons. But Sir Gilbert was most interested in hearing more about her fellow bunnies.

"Did you say a *dance* competition?" he asked incredulously. Peck was in the middle of a story about how she had pranked one of the dance squads by hiding glitter pouches under the wings of their fairy costumes. (The prank had helped the squad win; the judges were wowed by the colorful bursts of glitter when the bunnies had spread their wings at the end of the routine.)

"Oh yes!" Peck grinned, brushing

her bangs out of her eyes. "At the annual costume ball. The competition is *fierce*. We bunnies are excellent dancers." To prove her point, she hopped extra high and spun midair, striking a pose when she landed.

Sir Gilbert chuckled. "That much is obvious. Have you . . ." He stopped, placing a large paw gently on Peck's shoulder. She froze at his side, ears twitching.

"I hear it," she whispered. "Sounds like . . ."

The two Alphas finished the thought at the same time.

"Phantoms."

The sound was coming from the other side of a hill just up ahead. Sir Gilbert and Peck crept cautiously through the yellow grass to the top, peering around a few dry shrubs at the scene below.

A solitary baobab tree stood in the middle of the field. The trunk was as wide as Alphas Hollow, but rather than being made up of dozens of intertwined roots, this trunk was straight and smooth. It rose high into the air, branches sprawling out only at the very top. Even from this distance, Sir Gilbert and Peck could tell the leaves were dried up and dying.

Three Phantoms circled the trunk, all staring up at the sky. One seemed to be calling orders, flailing two large, clunky tentacles at the other two as he shouted.

But the Phantoms weren't the only problem—a large purple-and-black cloud hovered ominously over the baobab tree, churning and emitting a low, thunderous sound.

"It's a Phantom portal," Peck

whispered. "The Phantoms opened it over that poor tree."

Sir Gilbert narrowed his eyes. "But for what purpose?"

Straightening up, Peck pulled out her Alpha Stone. "Why don't we go find out?" she said boldly. Sir Gilbert nodded in approval, and together they headed down the hill toward the baobab tree.

"You there!" Sir Gilbert bellowed, and the Phantoms all spun around. "Step away from that tree at once."

The Phantom with the two lumbering tentacles giggled, and one of his smaller tentacles fell in front of his eye. "Or what?" he sneered. "You obviously don't know who you're dealing with, tiger. I am Stench, the Phantom Queen's right-hand Phantom!"

"Second right-hand Phantom," another

Phantom interrupted. "Leach is first."

"We're both her right-hand Phantoms," Stench said sullenly. "Two equal right hands."

"The Phantom Queen has two right hands?" the third Phantom wondered. "I thought she had two regular tentacles."

Sir Gilbert and Peck exchanged a glance as the Phantoms began to argue among themselves. Slowly, the two Alphas moved closer to the tree. Peck noticed movement in the shrubs lining the tops of the surrounding hills, and she nudged Sir Gilbert.

"There might be more Phantoms," she whispered, nodding to the shrubs. "Someone is watching us."

Sir Gilbert narrowed his eyes and glanced at his Alpha Stone. "We are Alphas now," he replied in a low voice. "We can take them all on, if we must."

Stench whirled around and glared at the Alphas. "Stop right there!" he hollered, his tentacles flapping. "Not another step!"

Peck put her paws on her hips. "What are you doing to that tree?" she demanded.

Stench giggled again. "You'll see. Any second now . . ."

As they watched, the branches and leaves high overhead began to tremble and wither beneath the portal. Peck gasped as thin, curling wisps of gray began to seep out of the leaves.

"It's on fire!" she whispered frantically.

Sir Gilbert sniffed. "I don't believe that's smoke," he replied. "In fact, I would venture to guess that it's smog . . . but I don't understand where it's coming from."

Peck thought quickly. "Baobab trees store water inside their trunks," she remembered out loud. "The Phantoms must be using the portal to pollute that water, and now it's expelling smog. Oh, Sir Gilbert—they're going to infect all the baobab trees in the savanna!"

Sir Gilbert's eyes flashed. "Not if we have anything to say about it!"

He and Peck brandished their Alpha Stones, both focusing as hard as they could on summoning the natural forces of Jamaa. Around them, the wind picked up, rustling through the dry grass. Peck's heart soared. The Alpha Stones were working!

The Phantoms stared around, looking unnerved. Then the wind died down, and the grass fell still. After a moment, Stench started to snicker. The other two

Phantoms followed suit, and soon all three were cackling and flailing their tentacles wildly.

"This is what happens every time the animals of Jamaa try to work together!" Stench sniggered, holding his sides. "They fail!"

Peck's heart sank like a stone. Stench was right, she thought miserably. The Alpha Stones hadn't worked at all. Then she looked up at the dark swirling portal and had an idea.

"We didn't fail at all," she told Stench with the most confident smile she could muster. "Look at that storm cloud!"

The Phantoms stared up at the portal. Stench's eye widened. "Where did *that* come from?"

Sir Gilbert caught on to Peck's trick

immediately. "We summoned it, of course," he announced. "And more are on the way."

The second Phantom spoke up nervously. "Um, boss? Isn't that our portal?"

Stench blinked, then narrowed his eye. "I think I know what a portal looks like," he snapped. "I *am* the Phantom Queen's right-hand Phantom."

"Second right-hand," the second Phantom muttered.

The third Phantom looked frightened. "What should we do?"

"Well, it's going to start raining any second," Peck told them. "Clean, fresh rainwater!"

"Not to mention thunder," Sir Gilbert added. "And lightning!"

"We need to take cover!" Stench yelled, flailing his clunky tentacles. "Retreat!"

He sped off across the grass, his fellow Phantoms right behind him. And just as Peck had hoped, their portal followed them across the savanna.

"The storm cloud is chasing us!" she heard Stench yelp. "Move faster! Hurry!" His cries faded as the Phantoms disappeared over a distant hill, along with the portal.

Peck clapped her paws and beamed. "It worked!"

"That was quick thinking," Sir Gilbert told her, clearly impressed. "Very clever indeed. And look—the baobab tree already looks stronger!"

The Alphas squinted up at the tree, shading their eyes against the hazy sun. Indeed, the leaves already appeared greener and brighter, and the smog had vanished.

"That was amazing!"

"Wow!"

"Did you see that? They saved the baobab tree!"

"They beat the Phantoms!"

"*And* got rid of the portal!"

Sir Gilbert and Peck looked around, startled. All along the top of the hill behind them, bunnies were poking their heads up from the long yellow grass. Several tigers emerged from a thick cluster of shrubs.

"Don't be afraid, friends!" Sir Gilbert called, waving them forward. "The Phantoms are gone."

"How did you do that?" one tiger asked wonderingly. Peck and Sir Gilbert smiled at each other.

"By working together," Peck told the animals firmly. "It's the only way to defeat the Phantoms. And we won't give up until we've driven them all from Jamaa!"

"But if we're going to succeed," Sir Gilbert added, "we need your help. We need *all* animals—tigers, bunnies, koalas, pandas, monkeys, and wolves—to unite, to trust one another. Spread the word!"

A few tigers looked skeptical, and one bunny scrunched up his nose doubtfully. But most of the animals looked more optimistic and began chattering enthusiastically among themselves.

Peck danced a little jig. "Look how excited they are!" she told Sir Gilbert. "Mira and Zios were right. We really can save Jamaa!"

Before Sir Gilbert could respond, the doubtful-looking bunny approached them. "I appreciate what you just did," he said, tugging nervously at his light brown ears. "But did you say we have to trust the *wolves*?"

Peck nodded resolutely. "This land belongs to the wolves as much as it does to us bunnies," she said. "If we work with them, we can—"

"But what if the wolves are working with the Phantoms?" the bunny interrupted, his eyes darting around.

Sir Gilbert frowned deeply. "Why would you suspect such a thing?"

The bunny swallowed. "Well, I saw one, right before you two arrived. A wolf, a shady-looking one. Bluish gray, bushy white eyebrows. He was lurking around when the Phantoms opened the portal. But he didn't try to stop them, like you did. He just let them try to destroy that tree."

Peck's ears drooped. "Thanks for letting us know," she said softly.

Sir Gilbert waited until the bunny had hopped away before turning to Peck.

"It must have been Greely," he said in a low voice.

"It couldn't have been," Peck said, although she suspected the same thing. "Why would he just let the Phantoms open a portal? Why wouldn't he try to stop them?"

Sir Gilbert's nostrils flared. "I suppose we'll have to ask him when the rest of the Alphas reconvene."

"Speaking of, we should get back to the Hollow," Peck said, attempting to recapture the positivity they'd both felt a few minutes ago. "Hopefully the others have been just as successful!"

The two Alphas set off back down the path. Peck tried to focus on the fact that they had successfully driven the Phantoms away and inspired the tigers and bunnies of Appondale. It was a great first step, she told herself. Maybe they really could do what Mira and Zios believed they could do.

But the knowledge that Greely had been nearby and had done nothing to help followed Peck and Sir Gilbert back to Alphas Hollow like a storm cloud.

CHAPTER FIVE

Cosmo sighed as a hot breeze ruffled the daisy on top of his hat. He and Graham had tracked the oily streaks across the sands of Kimbara Outback, which had led them to the source of the problem. Several thick dark spikes rose up out of the ground, like the tips of a giant's pitchfork. The spaces between the spikes were tightly packed with hardened sludge.

"Those things are interfering with the

reservoir," Graham said, scratching his head. "The Phantoms' doing, I'd guess, from all the muck and mud and yuck."

"This reservoir supplied water to all of Kimbara Outback." Cosmo pointed behind them, where the oily streaks spread out in different directions. "These used to be freshwater streams! Now they're just spreading pollution."

The two Alphas surveyed the brown, murky water in dismay. Even if they managed to get rid of the spikes, releasing such polluted water would only cause even worse contamination.

Graham stroked his beard. "A purifier, perhaps?" he mumbled, inspecting the dam. "A bigger spick-and-spanner? I can build one that will clean the water once we dismantle the spikes. In fact, I might be able to modify this . . ."

Still rambling to himself, Graham set to work with his tools, making adjustments to his smog vacuum.

Cosmo had other ideas. Or rather, the plants did. He could sense them trying to tell him something. The grass around the reservoir was dry and crunchy, the shrubs brown and stiff . . . but not all the plants were dying.

Each and every succulent plant was bright green and sturdy. Cosmo even noticed yellow flowers blooming on a few of them. He hurried over to the nearest one and placed his ear close to its thorns.

"Hello there," he whispered. "You look perfectly healthy. What's your secret?"

Cosmo listened intently. Nearby, several monkeys huddled together and watched him, pointing and snickering. But a few seconds later, it was Cosmo who was laughing in delight.

"That's it! Of course!" he cried, hurrying over to Graham. "Graham, we don't need a purifier—the water inside is clean! They store freshwater!"

"Hmm?" Graham didn't look up from his work. "No thanks, I'm not thirsty."

"Oh, you're not listening. Aha—look!" Cosmo plucked a yellow flower from the plant behind Graham. "See? The succulents are drinking the water, and it's still clean."

Frowning, the monkey Alpha pushed his goggles up his nose. "But the water is right there," he said, gesturing to the reservoir. Here and there, patches of grass stuck out from the murky water. "It's clearly dirty."

"Your eyes are playing tricks on you, my friend!" Leaning down, Cosmo picked up a rock and tossed it into the reservoir. It landed with a soft thump . . . and sat there on the surface.

Graham blinked several times. "The rock is floating! A floating rock, my goodness! Or . . . wait . . . ah. It's not sinking."

"Because there's nowhere to sink!" Cosmo finished with a grin. "This is just a giant, muddy puddle, not the reservoir."

"Then where *is* the reservoir?" Graham looked around. Then his eyes lit up. "Of course! Underground!"

"Exactly!" Cosmo cried. "The succulents are drinking it right now, sucking it up like straws!" Then his smile fell. "But that means the Phantoms' spikes extend underground, too," he fretted. "How will we dismantle them now? Should we start digging?"

Now it was Graham's turn to laugh. "Dig? Dig, dig, dig. That's always animals' answer to everything. Is that what your friends the succulents would do?" Before Cosmo could respond, Graham bounded over to his smog vacuum. "Let's take a cue from them, shall we?"

Beaming, Cosmo hurried over to help. Together, the two Alphas set to work transforming the smog vacuum into a water vacuum. They spent the afternoon inserting the bamboo tubes into the sludge between the dark spikes, then using the copper coils to connect the tubes to the vacuum's engine.

As they worked, a large crowd of koalas

and monkeys gathered to watch. "You can help!" Graham called to them. "Drag that big log over here."

Several monkeys did as he asked, and the Alphas put them to work hollowing out the trunk with spades and saws. When it was finished, they drove the hollow trunk straight into the ground, breaking through the mud and muck the Phantoms had used to obstruct the water.

Cosmo and Graham hurried over to the engine, and the other animals stepped back.

"Here goes nothing!" Graham said, flipping the switch. The vacuum rumbled to life, and everyone stared expectantly at the opening of the hollow trunk.

For a few seconds, nothing happened. Then gallons and gallons of clear, sparkling water began to pour from the trunk. The animals cheered at the sight of the water flowing out into the streams, washing away the oily streaks and spreading out across the arid land.

Graham and Cosmo grinned at each other as the koalas and monkeys surrounded them, clapping them on the back and thanking them.

"It was Graham's invention," Cosmo told the koalas. "He's full of brilliant ideas!"

"But I never would have thought of this if Cosmo hadn't noticed the succulents," Graham informed the monkeys. "His connection with plants is astonishing!"

The two Alphas shook hands, pleased with a job well done.

"Let's head back to the Hollow," Cosmo said, and Graham nodded in agreement. They set off through the desert, leaving

the koalas and monkeys splashing and
laughing in the cool, clean streams.

Meanwhile, Liza had spent hours
walking the streets of Jamaa Township,
speaking to any animal that would listen.
Now a crowd had gathered around her in
the square. They listened quietly as she
told them all about the Alphas and their
goals, some looking interested, others
doubtful or even irritated.

"Mira and Zios believe that unity is
our best chance against the Phantoms,"
Liza said, smiling around at the pandas,
monkeys, koalas, bunnies, and tigers. "And
that is what I believe, too. There was once a
time in Jamaa when all the species lived in

harmony. If we're going to reclaim our land from this enemy, banding together is the first step!"

A tiger snorted disdainfully, and Liza turned to him. "Yes?" she asked, keeping her tone polite.

"I mean no offense," the tiger told her. "But the guardian spirits have already tried that, and it failed."

"That battle was a disaster, all right," one of the monkeys said with a scowl. "No thanks to you tigers, rushing into battle without giving a thought to what the rest of us were doing."

"You monkeys were no better!" a koala cried angrily. "Hogging all the vines to make a net, like that could possibly work against the Phantoms."

The monkey crossed her arms.

"Because lassos were so much cleverer?"

Bickering broke out among the animals, each species blaming the others for the disastrous battle. Liza took a deep breath and tried to focus on the encouraging words Mira and Zios had told her.

"I know the last battle didn't go well," she said loudly and clearly. "But we can't give up! Surely you understand that arguing among yourselves isn't doing any species any good?"

"You're right!" one of the bunnies said sourly. "This is pointless. We might as well give up."

The bunnies hopped away, and the monkeys swung themselves back up into the trees. Liza watched helplessly as the koalas and tigers also went their separate ways. Soon, only a few pandas were left.

"What you're doing is really admirable," one told Liza, smiling sadly. "But it's hard to imagine the animals of Jamaa will ever find a way to trust one another again."

Liza held her head high. "I know it's a great challenge," she agreed. "But please, promise me you'll keep trying."

The other pandas nodded in agreement, and Liza headed back to Alphas Hollow feeling despondent. But it wasn't just the failed attempt at rallying the animals that had her down.

What troubled her even more was that not a single wolf had even been present. Just like Greely had said, they stuck with their own kind. How could Liza possibly spread a message of hope and unity to such a mistrustful species?

CHAPTER SIX

Greely crept through the trees, trying to catch the electric scent of the Phantoms' portal over the smell of pine trees and grass. The breeze shifted, and Greely's nose burned slightly. Adjusting his course, he headed deeper into Sarepia Forest.

If Sir Gilbert and Peck hadn't shown up in Appondale and ruined everything with their rash, reckless behavior, Greely thought dourly, he would already have the information he was looking for.

But there was no sense in feeling irritated. Greely had a job to do. He slowed, his eyes glinting as he caught sight of a purple glow in a clearing up ahead.

In fact, maybe the other Alphas' clumsy interference had actually worked to his advantage.

Greely peered through the dry, thorny bushes. Dozens of Phantoms filled the clearing, including Stench, who was looking abashed while a familiar Phantom with a particularly cruel sneer berated him.

"A storm cloud?" Leach seethed, gesturing to the portal Greely now saw hanging overhead. "You conjured that portal, you've done it countless times—

and some bunny convinced you it was a *storm cloud*?"

"Sorry, Leach," Stench mumbled. Before Leach could respond, the portal began to hum and crackle. Greely leaned as far forward as he dared, and it began to expand, sending little sparks shooting over the gathered Phantoms like fireworks. They hurried to the outskirts of the clearing and fell silent, watching and waiting. The humming noise grew into a dull roar, and then two enormous tentacles appeared, followed by a massive black blob covered in purple splotches.

The Phantom Queen had arrived.

Greely crouched, as still as a statue, and gazed at the colossal Phantom. The roar died down to a hum again, and the only other sound was the wind whistling through the canopy of pine needles overhead.

The Phantom Queen's pupil focused on Leach, who moved forward. A hissing, snapping crackle of energy passed between them like a static spark. Then Leach nodded and turned to face the other Phantoms.

"It's time for the final phase in our plan," Leach hissed, his eye shining with delight. "The Phantom Queen has directed us to launch an attack on Jamaa Township . . . in two days."

Greely watched the Phantoms cackle and rub their tentacles together gleefully. He would have to return to Alphas Hollow soon to warn the others. But his business here wasn't finished yet.

He crept farther into the clearing, listening intently as Leach whispered the Phantom Queen's plan, memorizing every word.

CHAPTER SEVEN

Thunder boomed loudly, and rain began to pitter-patter against the knotted trunk of Alphas Hollow. Inside, a few of the Alphas mumbled in their sleep. Only Peck was awake.

She'd volunteered to be the first to stay up on watch when everyone had started getting sleepy. Peck was still too energetic from their meeting to sleep. Her emotions were all over the place after hearing the other Alphas recount their adventures. Cosmo and Graham's success in Kimbara Outback had lifted Peck's spirits tremendously, and she'd beamed with pride when Sir Gilbert told the group how she'd tricked the Phantoms into leaving the baobab tree alone. Although privately, Peck couldn't help thinking it had been a close call. Mira and Zios had said their Alpha Stones would help give them power, so why weren't they able to do more?

Then Liza admitted she hadn't been so successful in Jamaa Township, and the celebratory mood had shifted. How were they ever going to get the animals to trust one another again? And where were all the wolves?

Where was *Greely*?

That was the big question. After seeing

his empty cushion at the round table, Peck and Sir Gilbert now informed the others what the bunny and told them. An uncomfortable silence followed their story.

Peck was so lost in thought, she didn't notice the light scratching sound at first. Then another clap of thunder caused her to jump, and she stared at the door.

Scratch. Scritch-scritch. Scraaatch.

Heart racing, Peck zoomed around the Hollow. "Wake up, wake up!" she cried, rousing Sir Gilbert first. "Someone's found us!"

The Alphas sprang into action, grabbing metal tools and spicy herbs and anything that could be used for protection.

"It's possible the Phantoms noticed our activity," Sir Gilbert said in a low voice, creeping toward the door. "They may have tracked us here. Prepare for battle . . ."

Peck held her breath, brandishing a paintbrush with extra-pointy bristles over her head and watching Sir Gilbert place his paw on the gnarled knob. Thunder rumbled as the entrance twisted and shifted open to reveal a shadowy figure in the rain. Lightning flashed in the distance, and Peck gasped.

"Greely!"

The wolf stepped inside, shaking water from his fur. "We should have a password for entry," he said shortly. "Getting in was far too easy. And I highly doubt a paintbrush would do you much good against a Phantom," he added to Peck.

She lowered the brush, her cheeks warm. "Where have you been?" she demanded, lifting her chin defiantly.

"You know where he's been," Sir Gilbert told her, though his eyes never left Greely. "With the Phantoms."

"Now, hold on," Liza said calmly. "Let's give Greely a chance to explain."

"Explain why he stood by and watched the Phantoms nearly destroy an innocent baobab tree?" Cosmo's hat slipped to the side when he shook his head. "There is no excuse for that."

"We don't have time for this." Greely looked around at the Alphas, his face mostly hidden in shadows. "The Phantoms are launching a final attack on Jamaa Township in two days' time."

Peck gasped, and the others immediately began talking all at once. Though their unease was apparent, it was obvious no one was ready to trust Greely's word, either.

"We need to strike first," Greely went on, ignoring the chatter. "Take the fight to the Phantoms before they can bring it to us."

Sir Gilbert's nostrils flared. "And if we do, whose side will you be fighting on?"

Greely arched a brow. "I'm not here to convince you to trust me. If you don't believe me . . ." He turned to leave. "That is on you."

Peck tugged anxiously at her ears. Greely couldn't possibly be on the Phantoms' side, could he? Jamaa belonged to the wolves just as much as any of the other animals. But before she could say anything, Cosmo called out. *"Wait!"*

All eyes turned to the koala Alpha. His amber eyes were wide and unfocused, his head tilted as if he was listening to something no one else could hear. Peck realized the rain and thunder had stopped. The sudden silence was eerie.

"The trees," he whispered. "The trees are crying for help."

Greely's nose twitched, and his pupils contracted. "Smoke," he hissed, then lunged for the entrance, the other Alphas right behind him.

Outside the Hollow, the air was thick with smoke. Peck coughed and covered her mouth with her paw, squinting through the haze. In the distance, the tops of the trees glowed orange.

"Fire!" she cried, pointing.

Without hesitation, the Alphas sprinted through the woods as a pack. The edge of Jamaa Township was ablaze, and they could hear the screams and shouts of the panicked animals. Many were pointing at the sky, and with a feeling of dread, Peck looked up.

Dozens of Phantoms swirled and twirled over the trees, fanning the flames. Every few seconds, a flash of light streaked through the highest branches, adding more fuel to the fire.

The Alphas tried to help, but each had a different idea about what should be done. Liza attempted to calm the frightened animals and help them escape in an orderly fashion, but Sir Gilbert tried to rally them into fighting the Phantoms with him. Graham quickly constructed a makeshift slingshot from brambles and rubber bands and tried to use it to frighten the Phantoms off, but Cosmo accidentally knocked the slingshot out of Graham's hands when he found a bucket of water and tossed it a little too enthusiastically.

We need to work together, Peck thought, and she caught Greely's eye.

"Our Alpha Stones!" She waved hers high in the air, doing her best to raise her voice over the noisy chaos. "We should use them!"

Greely glanced up at the Phantoms, his doubt evident. "You and Sir Gilbert tried that already," he reminded her, though he took his Alpha Stone out as well. "I saw your attempt. It failed."

"Then we'll just have to try again," Peck said desperately. "All six of us. It's our only chance!"

Turning, she stared up at the swirling

Phantoms and burning trees and focused. Greely did the same, and soon, a wind began to pick up just like it had in Kimbara Outback.

"Keep it going!" Peck called. "Everyone, *use your Alpha Stones*!"

One by one, the other Alphas followed suit. Cosmo clutched his Alpha Stone, and the next bucket of water he threw on the fire seemed to triple in volume, dousing the trees faster than the Phantoms could light them. Sparks erupted from Graham's slingshot like fireworks the moment his fingers wrapped around his Alpha Stone, sending several Phantoms fleeing in fright. When Sir Gilbert and Liza grabbed hold of their Alpha Stones, the atmosphere seemed to shift.

The wind swept and wrapped

around the Alphas, creating a powerful funnel. Streams of water and fire whirled gracefully in alternating arcs, extinguishing the trees and turning the flames on the Phantoms. The other animals forgot their panic and watched in awe as the Phantoms scattered.

When the last Phantom had vanished, the Alphas lowered their arms, and the wind died down. The flames fizzled out, and the water fell in gentle drops, putting out the last few burning leaves. For a moment, everything was still and silent.

Then the animals burst into cheers.

"We did it!" Peck beamed around at the other Alphas. "When we work *together*, we are unstoppable! The Phantoms are gone!"

"For now." Greely stared up at the sky, avoiding eye contact with the others.

"They'll be back in two days, and they'll be stronger."

"Which means we still have work to do," Liza said firmly.

Peck nodded, her whiskers quivering with excitement. "Then let's start planning!"

CHAPTER EIGHT

The sun began to rise over the treetops,
casting a golden glow over the leaves.
Inside Alphas Hollow, five exhausted but
determined leaders still sat around a table
covered in maps, notes, and photos. Cosmo
had brewed a pot of herbal tea to give them
energy as they planned through the night,
and now everyone's cups were cold and
mostly empty.

Tap-tap-tap. Tap, tap-tap. Tap. Tap.

"The secret knock," Peck said, hopping up immediately. "That's Liza."

She opened the entrance and stepped aside to let the panda Alpha in. Liza leaned her staff against the wall before taking her place at the table. Although she looked tired, she wore a pleased smile.

"I've spoken to each and every animal who witnessed what happened last night at Jamaa Township," she told the others. "And they've all agreed to join us in our attack against the Phantoms." Cosmo and Peck cheered, and Graham slapped his hands on the table in triumph.

"And," Liza added, her eyes sparkling, "several also volunteered to join us on our missions today to recruit more animals. I have a sign-up list here, so we can divide into groups based on species."

She slid the list to the center of the table so everyone could see. Peck leaned forward, delighted at the number of bunnies who had signed up. There were plenty of pandas, too, and tigers, koalas, monkeys . . .

But not a single wolf.

Deflated, Peck sat back down. She watched Greely out of the corner of her eye as he read the list, but his expression remained stony.

"Let's go over the plan once more," Sir Gilbert said. "After rallying as many animals as we can, we'll meet at midnight on the outskirts of the Phantom camp in Sarepia Forest—then launch a preemptive attack."

Greely reached forward and scratched an X in the center of the map. "The camp is located here." He paused, looking around the table. "Stealth is imperative," he told them. "If the Phantoms hear you lumbering through the bushes, you'll lose the element of surprise."

"*You?*" Sir Gilbert repeated. His voice was calm, but his eyes flashed like steel. "Don't you mean *us*? Or are you not planning on being a part of this endeavor?"

Graham frowned. "And why should we trust that what you say about the Phantoms is true? Why were you at their camp in the first place?"

"How do we know you'll bother trying to recruit the wolves?" Cosmo added. "We don't even know where the wolves *are*."

Greely's expression didn't change. "Their location is none of your concern, nor are my methods. I've done my part, and I'll continue to do so."

With that, he stood and headed for the door. The other Alphas exchanged worried glances, and Peck jumped up.

"I'll be right back," she said, then hurried after Greely.

Peck caught up to the wolf Alpha just outside of the Hollow. "Greely, wait," she said, putting a paw on his shoulder. "I just wanted to, um . . ."

Greely watched her impassively, and she took a deep breath. If there was one thing Peck had learned as an art teacher, it was that sometimes an animal just needed to know someone believed in them, especially when no one else did.

"I just wanted to tell you that I trust you," Peck said clearly. "I know you're on our side."

Blinking, Greely's eyes flickered back

to the twisted roots now concealing the entrance to the Hollow. When he finally responded, he didn't meet her gaze.

"Look for me in the battle."

Peck nodded, then watched as he disappeared into the woods without a sound.

CHAPTER NINE

In the heart of Sarepia Forest, the Phantom camp was buzzing with activity. Along the northern end of the clearing, a small group of Phantoms practiced melting rocks into thick, poisonous sludge. On the opposite end, a larger group was gathered around a pile of freshly dug dirt, which they were attempting to turn into oozy quicksand. And in the center of the camp, Leach was commanding a battalion of Phantoms standing in uniform rows.

"Spin!" he ordered, and the Phantoms began to twirl their tentacles in unison. Leach nodded approvingly. "Shock!" he yelled out, and sparks flew from their tentacles. "Smash!" Instantly, the Phantoms began pounding the ground in a heavy beat.

Stench drifted sullenly from one activity to the next. Leach had directed him to "supervise, but not participate in" the activities. It was, in Stench's opinion, highly unfair. He was the Phantom Queen's right-hand henchman, too—he should be able to give orders. But after his storm cloud mistake, Leach had threatened to have him demoted.

Pausing near the western end of the camp, Stench glanced up at the treetops, then did a double take. He could've sworn he'd seen something there. Two shiny orbs, like a pair of eyes.

Stench stared and stared, but the trees were still and dark. He scratched his head. Should he say something to Leach, just in case?

"Stench!" Leach yelled. "This is no time for stargazing! Get back to work!"

A few nearby Phantoms snickered, and Stench scowled. He skulked back over to the north end of the camp without looking back.

Along the eastern edge, the treetops quivered slightly as the monkeys readied their sturdy net made of straw and branches. Directly across the camp from them, the koalas hid in the leaves, each clutching their vine lassos. The tigers, bunnies, and pandas were spread out, covering the ground that surrounded the camp. Everyone crouched silently, tense and waiting for orders.

Five Alpha leaders huddled together at the northern edge as midnight approached. Sir Gilbert watched the moon rise higher, his nostrils flaring.

"We can't wait for Greely much longer," he said in a low voice. "It's only a matter of time before one of the Phantoms spots us, and then we lose the element of surprise."

"What if he isn't coming?" Cosmo couldn't help but ask. "What if . . . what if he's betrayed us? This could all be a trap!"

"It's not!" Peck whispered fiercely. "Greely will be here, I know it."

But as the minutes passed, even Peck's

hope began to fade. Graham shifted from foot to foot, and Cosmo eyed the horizon nervously. At last, Liza sighed.

"I think Sir Gilbert is right," she said bracingly. "If we're going to get the jump on them, we need to do it now."

The others nodded, some more reluctantly than others. Raising his paw, Sir Gilbert signaled to the monkeys and koalas in the treetops. Then he stood tall, rising above the bushes, and roared:

"Charge!"

Overhead, the koalas swung their lassos and pulled several surprised Phantoms, including Leach, high up into the air. Then the monkeys launched their nets in perfect coordination, trapping the remaining Phantoms on the ground. With roars and calls, paws and claws, the Alphas and other animals raced into battle together.

Leach snarled as the leaders raced toward the net. *"Spin!"* he screeched, and the Phantoms instantly obeyed. Their tentacles were a blur, whipping at the nets and lassos until they were free.

A thick smog seeped into the camp when several Phantoms began to swirl over the trees. The monkeys and koalas lashed out again with their nets and lassos, but the Phantoms defended themselves with electric sparks. Other Phantoms, including Leach, twirled over the quicksand pit, which steadily grew larger and larger, forcing the animals to the outskirts of the camp. The smog grew thicker, making it harder for the animals to see their targets.

Stench spun around, unsure of what to do. He noticed a cluster of bushes shaking, and the next thing he knew, a giant creature lumbered out of the woods, barreling straight for him.

"Monster! Monster!" Stench shrieked, flapping his tentacles and running in circles.

"Make way, make way!" Graham hollered from behind the creature—which wasn't a creature at all, but his newly designed super smog vacuum. Two pandas and a tiger helped him push the contraption as close to the edge of the quicksand as they dared. Five bunnies climbed to the top of the vacuum, each holding an extra-long bamboo tube.

"Here we go!" Graham called, then flipped the switch. With a growl that sent Stench scurrying away in fright, the vacuum rumbled to life. The bunnies clung to their tubes, slowly but surely sucking the smog from the air.

"Aha, I see you now!" Cosmo tossed his lasso, which landed neatly around Stench just before he reached the woods. The Phantom henchman yelped as Cosmo pulled him back into the fray.

And so the battle raged for hours, with neither side showing signs of giving up.

Suddenly, the super smog vacuum lurched to the side, sending the bunnies tumbling. "The quicksand!" Liza cried, hurrying over to help. "Graham, the vacuum is sinking!"

Several monkeys and pandas rushed to help pull the contraption away from the quicksand. Sir Gilbert had nearly reached them when a strange yet somehow familiar movement in the sky caught his eye.

"Look up!" The tiger Alpha's roar rose above the din of the battle. "Stop them!"

The other animals tilted their heads back and stared in horror at the Phantoms still swirling over the trees. The vacuum had cleared enough smog that now they could see a small purplish cloud, growing bigger by the second, raining down sparks.

Peck's stomach dropped when she realized what was happening.

"It's a portal!" she shouted frantically. "They're opening a portal!"

Lassos and stones flew through the air as the animals attempted to stop the Phantoms. But it was too late.

The Phantom Queen's tentacles emerged first, lowering slowly from the portal. Next came her body, her massive eye glaring right at the Alphas. The quicksand beneath her began to churn, sending the animals stumbling farther back. Graham's super smog vacuum sputtered to a halt, sinking deeper into the quagmire.

It's over, Peck realized in horror. *We've lost.*

Just then, a howl filled the air. Turning, Peck saw the full moon descending over the hill that sloped down into the camp. And on top of the hill . . .

"Greely," she whispered. And then, beaming, she shouted: *"Greely!"*

The Alpha leaders turned as Greely howled again. Another howl joined his, then another, and soon even the Phantoms were spinning around to look.

"The wolves!" Liza cried with joy. "He brought the wolves!"

Sir Gilbert gave a mighty roar, joined by his fellow tigers. The other animals whooped and called when Greely let out one final howl, then raced down the hill, his pack close behind him.

The wolves jumped into the fray, and with renewed energy and hope, the six remaining species of Jamaa fought together against the Phantoms. They used lassos and nets to slow the spinning Phantoms, and soon the smog began to lift and the quicksand's churning slowed.

But the Phantom Queen continued to descend from the portal. Her eye locked on to Sir Gilbert, who glared back. All around the camp, the other Alphas turned to look.

Wind whipped through the trees, and the animals moved back as the wind turned into a funnel that surrounded the portal. The quicksand hardened back into packed dirt, and the Alphas gathered closer together in the center. Directly above them, the Phantom Queen struggled to continue her descent.

The Alphas stood in a tight circle, back to back, feeling the power of their Alpha Stones surge through them. One by one, the Phantoms were sucked up into the portal, flailing their tentacles but finding nothing to grab onto. Leach was the last to vanish, leaving just the Phantom Queen.

The sun began to rise on the eastern

horizon, highlighting two figures above the trees. A fresh, cool wind swept down, and the Alphas all turned, squinting against the light.

"Mira!" Liza gasped. "And Zios!"

"You've done it!" Mira called to them, spreading her wings and soaring overhead. "You've harnessed your full power as Alphas!"

"And you've given all of Jamaa newfound strength," Zios boomed. "Including Mira and me. Hold fast, now . . ."

The guardian spirits of Jamaa seemed to radiate, strengthening the rays of early morning sun and filling the animals with renewed hope and warmth. The portal began to crackle and smoke, and slowly, the Phantom Queen retreated.

"It's working!" Sir Gilbert called to the

others, the powerful wind carrying his voice to the animals watching from the outskirts of the camp. "Steady now!"

Mira and Zios concentrated their powers on the portal. Slowly, the purplish-black swirling cloud began to shrink, emitting a few final sparks. The Phantom Queen's giant eye disappeared, and soon just the tips of her tentacles were visible.

"We've got her!" Mira cried, her feathers glowing gold in the sunrise. "Stay strong!"

One tentacle vanished, and the Alphas focused their power harder than ever. The portal shrank even more, and the Phantom Queen was going, going . . . *gone*.

The Alphas stared at the now empty portal, which was quickly fading. Peck was the first to speak.

"We did it," she said with a shaky laugh. "I can't believe it. We *did* it!"

"You did," Mira said warmly, and the Alphas turned to gaze at her. "Thank you, Alphas. Your—"

Suddenly, a long tentacle lashed out of the portal. It wrapped around Zios, pulling him into the churning cloud.

"No!" Mira's cry of distress rang throughout the forest, and she dived into the portal after him. The Alphas cried out in shock as the heron wrestled with the Phantom Queen's tentacle, trying desperately to free Zios. The portal swirled faster, rapidly shrinking around the guardian spirits of Jamaa . . .

With a ferocious growl, Greely leaped after them. But in a final spark, the portal closed behind Mira. The wolf Alpha's paws hit the ground, and he stared up at the clear sky in shock.

The wind died down to a gentle breeze. The Alphas stood in the clearing, all gazing in disbelief at the spot where the portal had been. The Phantoms were gone.

But so were the guardian spirits of Jamaa.

Cosmo blinked, a tear trickling down his cheek. "There must be a way to bring them back. Right?"

"We don't know where the portal leads," Peck said, her throat tight. "They're . . . they're lost."

Before anyone could respond, a panda exclaimed:

"They did it! The Alphas saved us!"

"The Phantoms are gone!" a bunny squeaked, hopping up and down.

Next to her, a tiger stepped forward. "Jamaa is ours once again!"

The animals burst into cheers, crowding around the Alphas and clapping them on the shoulders. Even the wolves joined the celebration, politely shaking paws with the other animals. After a moment, Liza smiled sadly at her fellow leaders.

"They're right," she said. "We saved Jamaa. And we couldn't have done it without Zios and Mira."

Sir Gilbert nodded solemnly. He raised his paw, and a hush fell over the animals.

"A moment of silence," he said. "For the lost guardian spirits of Jamaa." He paused, looking around at each of the leaders. "Once this land is restored, we will find them. No matter what it takes."

As one, the tigers, pandas, bunnies, koalas, monkeys, and wolves bowed their heads in remembrance and gratitude. And overhead, the sun rose higher in the clear blue sky: a new day in Jamaa.

CHAPTER TEN

"Found the last copper coil!"

Cosmo burst out of the bushes near Alphas Hollow, waving the coil over his head. Near the entrance, Graham beamed.

"Excellent, perfect, thank you!" he exclaimed, taking the coil from Cosmo. "I think we managed to salvage all the parts."

The two Alphas shook paws, then entered the Hollow together.

Inside, the other Alphas chatted animatedly while they worked. Sir Gilbert and Liza were adding notes to each other's maps, deep in conversation about which areas of Jamaa had been most damaged by the Phantoms. Greely examined the books on the shelf near the fireplace, while Peck packed all the art supplies she could carry, rambling about the millions of new projects she had in mind.

"Oh!" she squeaked, dropping a tube of paint. Greely looked down at his gray fur, now sprayed with specks of yellow. "I'm so sorry!" Peck handed him a towel, her cheeks a deep purple.

Greely sniffed. "It's nothing," he murmured, taking the towel. But Peck could have sworn she caught the hint of a smile on his face. Grinning, she went back to bundling her paintbrushes.

Nearly an hour later, the Alphas had finished their packing. Liza tossed a pail of water on the fireplace, putting the flames out with a final hiss. Silence fell as the Alphas gathered around the table.

Sir Gilbert cleared his throat. "The Phantoms may be gone, but there is much cleaning to do to restore Jamaa—and missing Heartstones to find."

"There will be fences that need mending with each species we bring back," Liza mused. "I'll be focusing on helping those animals acclimate to Jamaa, and to one another."

"So much of the land is still too polluted for habitation," Peck said. "Many animals will have to leave until it's clean. When they come to Jamaa Township, I'd like to be there to welcome them and help them settle in until their homes are safe to return to."

Graham clutched a stack of papers to his chest. "I've drawn out designs for my super smog vacuum," he told the Alphas. "So others can build their own. I'm also working on a gadget that can purify water, something I can bring to Crystal Sands when it's ready."

"Speaking of water," Cosmo said, smiling at his friend, "I'm returning to Kimbara Outback to check on the reservoir and continue my medical work." He held up a satchel stuffed with herbs and leaves he'd collected from the forest. "Lots of new ingredients to work with!" He turned to Sir Gilbert, who was holding a rolled-up map. "And where will you go?"

"To search for the missing Heartstones," Sir Gilbert said. "Liza and I have marked the areas where some Heartstones are rumored to be hidden—I'll start there, and I have a team of tigers and pandas who have offered to join me." He raised an eyebrow at Greely. "The wolves are welcome to come along as well."

Greely tilted his head slightly. "I, too, plan on tracking down the Heartstones. But while I appreciate your invitation, I work better alone."

"As you wish," Sir Gilbert replied. "Perhaps it would be more effective this way. We'll cover more ground."

"Well then." Liza smiled, though her eyes were shining with tears. "I suppose this is goodbye, for now."

"We'll see each other again," Peck said firmly. "I'm sure of it."

"Absolutely!" Cosmo agreed, and Graham nodded. After a moment, Greely dipped his head slightly in acknowledgment.

"I suppose that wouldn't be the worst thing," he said drily, causing Peck to giggle.

Sir Gilbert's eyes softened as he looked around the group. "It's been an honor working with all of you," he said. "Best of luck on your missions."

Handshakes and hugs followed, then the Alphas left their Hollow together. The massive trunk trembled slightly, the roots twisting and shifting until the entrance was concealed. And then the magnificent tree was dormant once more, waiting for the day the Alphas would return.

EPILOGUE

Many Years Later . . .

As the first stars appeared in the vast sky over Appondale, Sir Gilbert rose from his spot beside a crackling campfire. Bidding his cheetah friends good night, he withdrew to the makeshift den he'd arranged. Curling up on a soft mat, Sir Gilbert soon fell fast asleep.

But hours later, the tiger Alpha awoke suddenly. His ears twitched as he slowly sat up, listening intently. He'd heard something, he was sure of it. And then:

"Sir Gilbert?"

The ethereal voice was barely audible, but Sir Gilbert would recognize it anywhere.

"Mira," he breathed, straining to hear more.

"Sir Gilbert, we need your help . . ."

A light breeze ruffled Sir Gilbert's fur, and he stood. For years, he'd worked hard to retrieve dozens of missing Heartstones and to restore peace to this land. Now, it seemed, the time had come for his next mission.

He had to find the lost guardian spirits and bring them back to Jamaa.

CONTINUE YOUR
ANIMAL JAM
ADVENTURE!

The story continues online! Uncover this book's code to unlock more fun on www.animaljam.com! Find the letters and numbers engraved on the stones at the beginning of each chapter and decipher them using the code below. Make sure to keep the letters and numbers in the right order of chapters one through ten!

Once you solve the code, go to www.animaljam.com/redeem or the Play Wild app to redeem your code!*

CODE

Replace	1	i	b	e	d	j
With	A	B	C	D	E	F
Replace	r	n	c	q	l	p
With	G	H	I	J	K	L
Replace	g	5	h	t	m	y
With	M	N	O	P	Q	R
Replace	3	s	f	o	k	v
With	S	T	U	V	W	X
Replace	u	2	a	x	z	w
With	Y	Z	1	2	3	4

Each code valid for a one-time use.